MAGIC POSTCARDS

A Postcard from Australia

Written by Laurie Friedman

Illustrated by Roberta Ravasio

A Blossoms Beginning Readers Book

CRABTREE
Publishing Company
www.crabtreebooks.com

BLOSSOMS BEGINNING READERS LEVEL GUIDE

Level 1 Early Emergent Readers Grades PK-K
Books at this level have strong picture support with carefully controlled text and repetitive patterns. They feature a limited number of words on each page and large, easy-to-read print.

Level 2 Emergent Readers Grade 1
Books at this level have a more complex sentence structure and more lines of text per page. They depend less on repetitive patterns and pictures. Familiar topics are explored, but with greater depth.

Level 3 Early Readers Grade 2
Books at this level are carefully developed to tell a great story, but in a format that children are able to read and enjoy by themselves. They feature familiar vocabulary and appealing illustrations.

Level 4 Fluent Readers Grade 3
Books at this level have more text and use challenging vocabulary. They explore less familiar topics and continue to help refine and strengthen reading skills to get ready for chapter books.

School-to-Home Support for Caregivers and Teachers

This book helps children grow by letting them practice reading. Here are a few guiding questions to help the reader with building his or her comprehension skills. Possible answers appear here in red.

Before Reading:
• What do I think this story will be about?
  • *I think this story will be about Camila and Carlos visiting Australia.*
  • *I think this story will be about the kangaroos and koalas that the twins will see.*

During Reading:
• Pause and look at the words and pictures. Why did the character do that?
  • *I think Jack wanted the twins to see the Great Barrier Reef because it is the biggest coral reef in the world.*
  • *I think Camila and Carlos enjoyed snorkeling with Jack because they were able to see the colorful reef and fish, as well as turtles swimming.*

After Reading:
• Describe your favorite part of the story.
  • *My favorite part was when the seals were wriggling on their bellies.*
  • *I liked seeing the pictures of the Great Barrier Reef and the many beaches.*

Camila and Carlos stood in front of their mailbox.

"Your turn," said Carlos.

Slowly, Camila opened the mailbox.

Another postcard!

She read it out loud to
her brother.

Dear
Camila and Carlos,
Hold this card.
Close your eyes.
Count to ten.
Wait for a surprise.
See you soon!

Jack

"Where are we going?" asked Carlos.

Camila turned the postcard over.

A map of Australia was on the back.

Camila and Carlos were going to Australia!

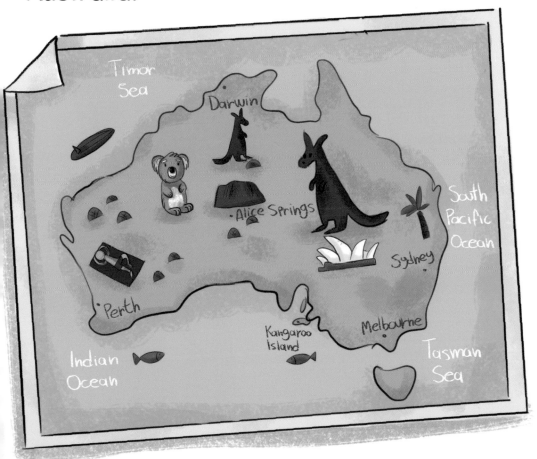

"Ready?" asked Camila.

Carlos nodded. Camila and Carlos held the postcard.

They closed their eyes and counted.

One
Two
Three
Four
Five
Six
Seven
Eight
Nine
Ten

Camila and Carlos opened their eyes.

They were on a ferry.

"Welcome to Australia!" said a boy. "My name is Jack."

"You're in Sydney," he told them. "It's the largest city in Australia."

Jack pointed to a bridge.

"That's the Sydney Harbour Bridge, one of the most famous sites in Sydney.

It's called the Coat Hanger because of its shape."

Then he pointed to another famous site—the Sydney Opera House.

"It looks like a sailboat," said Camila. She took a picture.

Sydney Opera House

Camila and Carlos saw the sites of Sydney from the ferry.

Jack told them more about Australia.

"Australia is both a country and a continent," said Jack.

"There are big cities in Australia.

But also beautiful beaches, dry deserts, and some pretty cool animals."

"We'll see them all—but first, lunch!" said Jack.

He took Carlos and Camila to a restaurant on the harbor.

Camila ate all her crispy fish and chips.

A hungry seagull ate one of Carlos's chips!

It was time to see other sites.

Jack told Camila and Carlos their postcard would take them from place to place.

Camila and Carlos held the postcard and closed their eyes.

When they opened them, they were on a beach.

"Australia is an island. It's surrounded by water.

That means there are lots of beaches in Australia!" said Jack.

He told Camila and Carlos he loved coming to the beach.

It didn't take long to figure out why.

Camila and Carlos played in the water.

Then they learned how to surf.

When they were done, Jack took them for a treat.

Fairy floss.

Camila giggled. "We call it cotton candy."

Carlos couldn't talk. His mouth was full!

It was time to see the Australian outback.

Camila and Carlos held their postcard and closed their eyes.

When they opened them, they were in a desert. Riding on camels!

"The dry, desert areas of Australia are called the outback," said Jack.

"Most people in Australia live in coastal cities, like Sydney.

But there's a lot of history in the outback."

Camila, Carlos, and Jack rode over red sand dunes.

They toured a large rock formation called Uluru.

"Uluru was formed millions of years ago," said Jack.

"For many people, this land is a sacred place."

Jack took Carlos and Camila to a small market to shop.

Camila filled a basket with painted rocks.

Carlos picked out a rainstick.

When he moved the rainstick it made a sound like falling rain.

Rainsticks

Dot technique on rock

Basket

Camila took pictures of beautiful handmade arts and crafts.

Camila and Carlos wanted to stay longer.

But there was more of Australia to see.

They held their postcard and blinked.

"Welcome to Kangaroo Island!" said Jack.

"Time to see some animals."

"YAY!" said Camila and Carlos.

Carlos and Camila saw kangaroos.

"Kangaroos carry their babies in pouches," said Jack.

He told them a baby kangaroo is called a joey.

Camila and Carlos saw koalas in trees.

Some were playing. Some were sleeping. Some were eating leaves.

"They're so cute!" said Carlos.

Carlos, Camila, and Jack went to another beach.

Camila took pictures of seals wriggling on their bellies.

Sea Lions

And sea lions using their flippers to move across the sand.

Jack had one last place to show Camila and Carlos.

The Great Barrier Reef.

"This is the biggest coral reef in the world," said Jack.

"Want to take a look underwater?"

"YES!" said Carlos and Camila.

27

They put on their snorkeling gear and went into the water.

Carlos and Camila saw bright, colorful reefs.

They saw all sorts of fish. Even turtles!

When they came out of the water,
the Sun was starting to set.

It was time to return home.

"Thank you for showing us your country," Camila and Carlos said.

"I hope you will come back one day," said Jack.

Camila and Carlos promised to return.

Then they held their postcard and closed their eyes.

Camila and Carlos were back home.

With happy memories of their special day in Australia.

ABOUT THE AUTHOR

Laurie Friedman is the award-winning author of more than seventy-five critically acclaimed picture books, chapter books, and novels for young readers, including the bestselling *Mallory McDonald* series and the *Love, Ruby Valentine* series. She is a native Arkansan, and in addition to writing, loves to read, bake, do yoga, and spend time with her friends and family. For more information about Laurie and her books, please visit her website at www.lauriebfriedman.com.

ABOUT THE ILLUSTRATOR

Roberta Ravasio was born in a farmhouse in Bergamo, Italy. She attended the high school of arts in her city and later moved to Milan, where she completed the School of Comics. In her work she uses a combination of traditional and digital media, and creates characters, greeting cards, books, and more. When she is not drawing, she loves playing with her son, running, and watching TV dramas.

CRABTREE
Publishing Company

Written by: Laurie Friedman

Illustrations by: Roberta Ravasio

Art direction and layout by: Rhea Wallace

Series Development: James Earley

Proofreader: Melissa Boyce

Educational Consultant: Marie Lemke M.Ed.

Library and Archives Canada
Cataloguing in Publication

CIP available at Library and Archives
Canada

Library of Congress Cataloging-in-
Publication Data

CIP available at Library of Congress

Crabtree Publishing Company

www.crabtreebooks.com   1-800-387-7650

Printed in the U.S.A./CG20210915/012022

Published in the United States
Crabtree Publishing
347 Fifth Avenue, Suite 1402-145
New York, NY, 10016

Published in Canada
Crabtree Publishing
616 Welland Ave.
St. Catharines, ON, L2M 5V6